This book belongs to:

. . . .

. . . .

Quarto is the authority on a wide range of topics.

Quarto educates, entertains and enriches the lives of our readers—enthusiasts and lovers of hands-on living.

www.quartoknows.com

Publisher: Maxime Boucknooghe

Editorial Director: Victoria Garrard

Art Director: Miranda Snow

Series Designer: Victoria Kimonidou

Designer: Chris Fraser

Editor: Joanna McInerney

© 2017 Quarto Publishing plc

First Published in 2017 by QED Publishing,
an imprint of The Quarto Group.
The Old Brewery, 6 Blundell Street,
London N7 9BH, United Kingdom.
T (0)20 7700 6700 F (0)20 7700 8066
www.QuartoKnows.com

A catalogue record for this book is available from the British Library.

ISBN 978 1 78493 955 7

Manufactured in Huizhou, China TL102017

9 8 7 6 5 4 3 2 1

Snow White and the Very Angry Dwarf

Written by Steve Smallman

Illustrated by Neil Price

Once upon a time there was a young girl called Snow White. She was lovely, but the Wicked Queen was jealous and wanted to get rid of her.

The queen's magic mirror told her that Snow White was prettier than she was and she wasn't having that!

Snow White ran away. She came across a little cottage.
Nobody was home, but the door was unlocked so she crept inside.

There were seven little chairs around a low table in
the kitchen and seven little beds in the bedroom upstairs.

"Oh my goodness!" cried Snow White. "Seven darling little
children must live here with no one to look after them."

The cottage was a mess so Snow White set to work tidying,

sweeping,

polishing... and singing so sweetly that all the animals in the forest came to listen!

"There," she sighed, "clean as a whistle!"

Soon after, Snow White heard
footsteps outside. "The children are back!
Come on in my little poppets," she cried
flinging open the door...

...only to be greeted
by six bearded little men!

"Oh, who are you?" asked Snow White.

"I'M SHOUTY,"

"I'm Hairy,"

"I'm Hungry,"

"I'm
Whiffy,"

PARP!

and "I'm Jolly!"

"I'm Sniffy,"

replied the dwarves.

"But... WHO ARE YOU?" they all asked.

"I'm Snow White. I was lost and I found your dear little cottage and I'm really sorry but I went in and I've tidied up and made some...

..."FOOD!" shouted the dwarves, and rushed past her to tuck in to the stew. Snow White told them her sad story while they ate.

The dwarves had almost
finished eating when another dwarf
stormed in looking very cross.
His name was Angry.

"Who is this?"
he shouted rudely.

"This is Snow White," said **Hungry**. "She's come
to stay and she's made us some lovely food."

"I'm sorry Angry but there's no stew left,"
said Snow White. "How about some cake instead?"

"What kind of cake?"
asked Angry.

"Cherry cake,"
replied Snow White.

"BUT I HATE
CHERRIES!"
shouted Angry.

Then he kicked over his chair and stormed out of
the cottage, slamming the door behind him.

"Oh my goodness!" cried Snow White. "Is he always like that?"

"YES!" replied the dwarves all together.

"HE ALWAYS SHOUTS AT ME BECAUSE I'M TOO NOISY!" shouted Shouty.

"He gets angry with me if he smells anything nasty and it's not always me!" said Whiffy.

SNIFF!

"He shouts (sniff) at me whenever I sniff. It's not my fault, (sniff) noses run in my family!" sniffed Sniffy.

"He gets cross with me when my tummy rumbles too loudly," mumbled Hungry.

"He goes mad just because I sometimes leave hair in the bath," replied Hairy.

"And he gets cross with me because I'm too cheerful. It makes me laugh and then he gets crosser!" chuckled Jolly.

tee-hee!

Snow White found Angry outside, bashing a tree trunk with a stick.

"What a clever idea to go off on your own when you're angry." said Snow White. "But instead of bashing a tree, why not collect some firewood?"

"I'd have a lot of wood!" grumbled Angry. "The other dwarves make me so cross!"

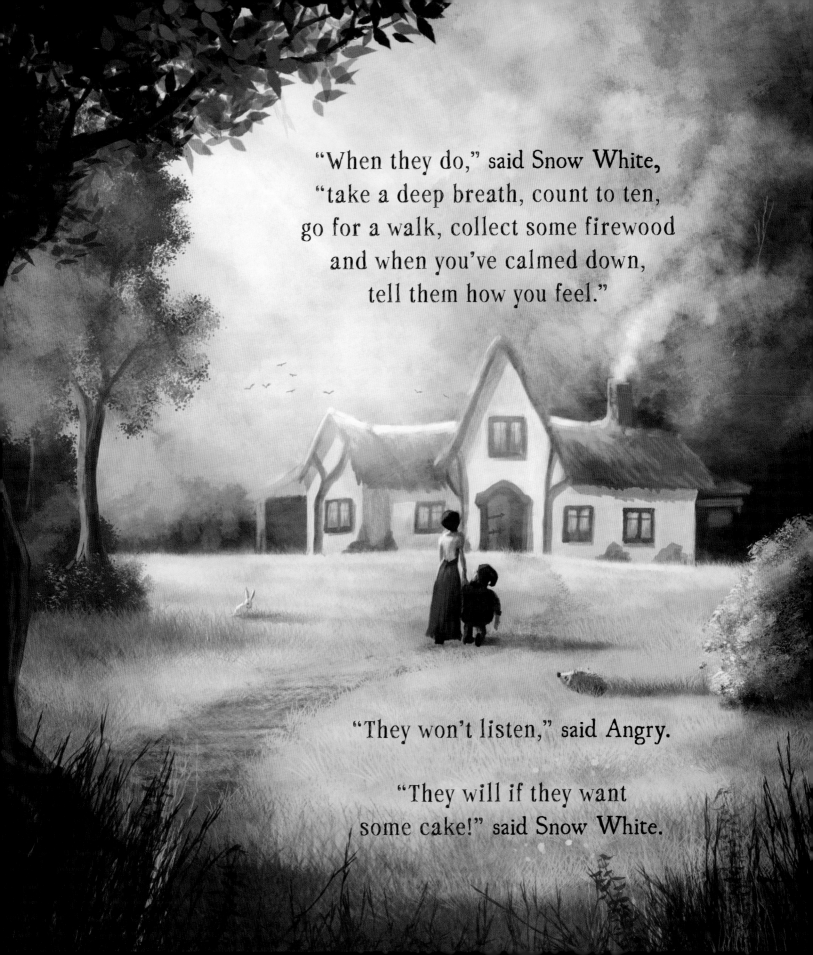

"When they do," said Snow White,
"take a deep breath, count to ten,
go for a walk, collect some firewood
and when you've calmed down,
tell them how you feel."

"They won't listen," said Angry.

"They will if they want
some cake!" said Snow White.

Back at the cottage, Angry explained to the
other dwarves why they make him so cross.

"You're always sniffing,
Sniffy. Couldn't you
try using a tissue?"

"Okay, (sniff)
I'll try, (sniff)"
sniffed Sniffy.

Snow White helped everybody to
say what they thought, and nobody
shouted, not even Shouty!

Angry said sorry to everyone and they all said
sorry back. Then they all had a group hug,
which Whiffy spoilt, just a bit.

PARP!

Angry was about to get cross when he remembered
what Snow White had told him. He didn't dare take
a deep breath so he went outside, counted to ten
and walked off to collect some wood.

Angry soon felt calmer, but he had collected so much
wood that he couldn't see where he was going and...

CRASH!

...he bumped into an old lady who fell on her bottom,
dropping the shiny red apple she was carrying. The apple
smashed to pieces, leaving a nasty black stain on the ground.

"YOU CLUMSY FOOL!" screeched the old lady, whose wig had fallen off. "It took me ages to make that poisoned apple for Snow White and now it's ruined!"

It was the Wicked Queen in disguise!

"We haven't got any apples, but you could have a piece of cherry cake if you like?" suggested Angry.

"I HATE CHERRIES!"
roared the queen.

"I think you should take a deep breath, count to ten, go for a walk, collect some wood and when you've calmed down, tell me how you feel." Angry calmly replied.

The Wicked Queen didn't appreciate Angry's advice, so she stomped off in a huff.

Snow White and the other dwarves came out
to see what all the shouting was about.

"Oh, Angry, thank you," cried Snow White.
"You got rid of that nasty Wicked Queen and
you didn't even lose your temper!"

Then she gave him a big piece of cherry cake
with all the cherries picked out.

Snow White and the seven dwarves went back to
the cottage where they lived fairly happily ever after.

And they never ran out of firewood again!

Next Steps

Show the children the cover again. When they first saw it, did they think that they already knew the story? How is this story different from the traditional story?

Angry was cross a lot of the time. Ask the children if they sometimes get cross. What sorts of things make them angry? How can they tell when they are feeling really cross?

Angry the dwarf did a lot of shouting and stomping about when he was angry. Is that kind of behaviour ok? How does it make others feel?

Snow White gave Angry suggestions to help him to calm down. What did she suggest? Ask the children which of those things they could do if they were feeling angry. Explain that there are lots of ways to deal with anger.

Angry managed not to lose his temper with the Wicked Queen. Do the children think he will ever get angry again? Is it ok to be angry sometimes? Discuss how it is important to talk about your feelings.

All the dwarves in this story have names that describe what they are like. Ask the children what they would be called if they were one of the dwarves.